BAHUBALI

IN THE THIRD CENTURY BC, MANY JAINA MONKS OF MAGADHA LEFT THE LAND OF THEIR ANCESTORS TO ESCAPE A SEVERE DROUGHT. THEY CROSSED THE VINDHYAS AND CAME DOWN TO SOUTH INDIA.

AS THE M... TO PLACE, BEAUTIFUL...

THEY CLIMBED A SMALL HILL...

...AND SAT DOWN TO MEDITATE.

THE TWO MONKS WERE CHANDRAGUPTA MAURYA, THE EMPEROR WHO HAD GIVEN UP THE THRONE OF MAGADHA, AND HIS GURU, BHADRA BAHU SWAMI. THE PLACE WHERE THEY FOUND PEACE AND QUIET TO MEDITATE WAS KALVAPU, TODAY KNOWN AS SHRAVANA BELAGOLA.

THE PRIEST BEGAN TO ANOINT THE IMAGE WITH MILK.

CHAVUNDARAYA WAS PLEASED WITH HIMSELF.

I HAVE ACHIEVED THE IMPOSSIBLE! I HAVE FULFILLED MY MOTHER'S WISH. I HAVE BROUGHT BAHUBALI TO HER. I HAVE BROUGHT HIM TO ALL THESE DEVOTEES HERE.

BUT HIS PRIDE WAS SHORT-LIVED.

WE HAVE BEEN POURING POTS AND POTS OF MILK. YET...

...THE MILK ONLY FLOWS DOWN TO THE WAIST OF BAHUBALI SWAMI. NO FARTHER.

STRANGE! MM-M-M!

A THOUSAND YEARS HAVE GONE BY. WE NOW HAVE A MOTORABLE ROAD FROM THE CITY OF BANGALORE TO SHRAVANA BELAGOLA.

WE HAVE HELICOPTERS TO SHOWER FLOWERS OVER BAHUBALI, OR GOMMATA AS HE IS NOW KNOWN, ON THE OCCASION OF MAHA-MASTAKA-ABHISHEKA, THE CEREMONY HELD ONCE IN TWELVE YEARS WHEN LAKHS OF DEVOTEES CONGREGATE TO WORSHIP HIM.

PEOPLE COME AND GO, BUT GOMMATA REMAINS MOTIONLESS, UNPERTURBED, SERENE, BRAVING ALL THE ELEMENTS.

THE ACK QUIZ
EPICS & MYTHOLOGY

1. Which god rides a crow?
2. Name Surya's charioteer.

3. Who are the two brothers in the image?
4. Which kingdom are they fighting for?
5. Which of these two brothers was an ally of Rama?

6. What is the name of Indra's weapon?
7. What is the name of his elephant?
8. What is the name of Indra's capital?

9. Who is the guru of the asuras?
10. The gods and asuras churned the ocean for _____.

ANSWERS: 1. Shani 2. Aruna 3. Vali and Sugriva 4. Kishkindha 5. Sugriva 6. Vajra 7. Airavata 8. Amaravati 9. Shukracharya 10. Amrit (Divine Nectar)

THE ACK QUIZ
EPICS & MYTHOLOGY

1 What is Parashurama's weapon?

2 Who were Krishna's birth parents?

3 Who is the person in the image?

4 Who was his mother?

5 Who was he married to?

6 Who is the woman in the image?

7 She is also known as Jahnavi. Which sage is she named after?

8 Which king brought her down to earth?

9 Manthara was the maid of which queen?

10 Who is Jatayu's brother?

ANSWERS
1. Axe 2. Devaki and Vasudeva 3. Abhimanyu 4. Subhadra 5. Uttara 6. Ganga 7. Jahnu 8. Bhagirath 9. Kaikeyi 10. Sampati